After recess, Treehorn was thirsty, so he went down the hall to the water bubbler. He couldn't reach it, and he tried to jump up high enough. He still couldn't get a drink, but he kept jumping up and down, trying.

His teacher walked by. "Why, Treehorn," she said. "That isn't like you, jumping up and down in the hall. Just because you're shrinking, it does not mean you have special privileges. What if all the children in the *school* started jumping up and down in the halls? I'm afraid you'll have to go to the Principal's office, Treehorn."

So Treehorn went to the Principal's office.

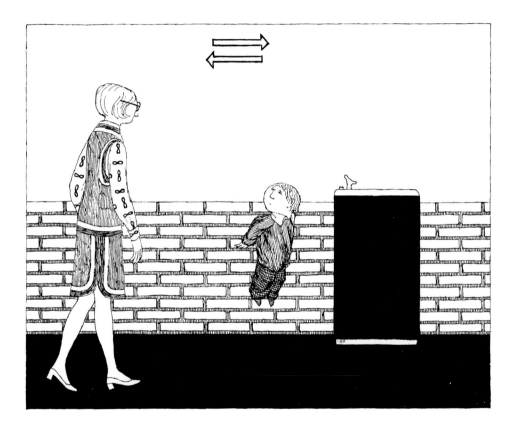

"I'm supposed to see the Principal," said Treehorn to the lady in the Principal's outer office.

"It's a very busy day," said the lady. "Please check here on this form the reason you have to see him. That will save time. Be sure to put your name down, too. That will save time. And write clearly. That will save time."

Treehorn looked at the form:

CHECK REASON YOU HAVE TO
SEE PRINCIPAL *(that will save time)*
☐ 1. Talking in class
☐ 2. Chewing gum in class
☐ 3. Talking back to teacher
☐ 4. Unexcused absence
☐ 5. Unexcused illness
☐ 6. Unexcused behavior

P.T.O.

There were many things to check, but Treehorn couldn't find one that said "Being Too Small to Reach the Water Bubbler." He finally wrote in "SHRINKING."

When the lady said he could see the Principal, Treehorn went into the Principal's office with his form.

The Principal looked at the form, and then he looked at Treehorn. Then he looked at the form again.

"I can't read this," said the Principal. "It looks like SHIRKING. You're not SHIRKING, are you, Treehorn? We can't have any shirkers here, you know. We're a team, and we all have to do our very best."

"It says SHRINKING," said Treehorn. "I'm shrinking."

"Shrinking, eh?" said the Principal. "Well, now, I'm very sorry to hear that, Treehorn. You were right to come to me. That's what I'm here for. To guide. Not to punish, but to guide. To guide all the members of my team. To solve all their problems."

"But I don't have any problems," said Treehorn. "I'm just shrinking."

"Well, I want you to know I'm right here when you need me, Treehorn," said the Principal, "and I'm glad I was here to help you. A team is only as good as its coach, eh?"

The Principal stood up. "Goodbye, Treehorn. If you have any more problems, come straight to me, and I'll help you again. A problem isn't a problem once it's solved, right?"

By the end of the day Treehorn was still smaller.

At the dinner table that night he sat on several cushions so he could be high enough to see over the top of the table.

"He's still shrinking," sniffed Treehorn's mother. "Heaven knows I've *tried* to be a good mother."

"Maybe we should call a doctor," said Treehorn's father.

"I did," said Treehorn's mother. "I called every doctor in the Yellow Pages. But no one knew anything about shrinking problems."

She sniffed again. "Maybe he'll just keep getting smaller and smaller until he disappears."

"No one disappears," said Treehorn's father positively.

"That's right, they don't," said Treehorn's mother more cheerfully. "But no one shrinks, either," she said after a moment. "Finish your carrots, Treehorn."

The next morning Treehorn was so small he had to jump out of bed. On the floor under the bed was a game he'd pushed under there and forgotten about. He walked under the bed to look at it.

It was one of the games he'd sent in for from a cereal box. He had started playing it a couple of days ago, but he hadn't had a chance to finish it because his mother had called him to come right downstairs that minute and have his breakfast or he'd be late for school.

Treehorn looked at the cover of the box:

THE *BIG* GAME
FOR KIDS TO GROW ON
IT'S TREMENDOUS! IT'S DIFFERENT!
IT'S FUN! IT'S EASY! IT'S COLOSSAL!
PLAY IT WITH FRIENDS!
PLAY IT ALONE!
Complete with Spinner, Board, Pieces,
and—!
COMPLETE INSTRUCTIONS!

The game was called THE *BIG* GAME FOR KIDS TO GROW ON.

Treehorn sat under the bed to finish playing the game.

He always liked to finish things, even if they were boring. Even if he was watching a boring program on TV, he always watched it right to the end. Games were the same way. He'd finish this one now. Where had he left off? He remembered he'd just had to move his piece back seven spaces on the board when his mother had called him.

He was so small now that the only way he could move the spinner was by kicking it, so he kicked it. It stopped at number 4. That meant he could move his piece ahead four spaces on the board.

The only way he could move the piece forward now was by carrying it, so he carried it. It was pretty heavy. He walked along the board to the fourth space. It said CONGRATULATIONS, AND UP YOU GO: ADVANCE THIRTEEN SPACES.

Treehorn started to carry his piece forward the thirteen spaces, but the piece seemed to be getting smaller. Or else *he* was getting *bigger.* That was it, he *was* getting bigger, because the bottom of the bed was getting close to his head. He pulled the game out from under the bed to finish playing it.

He kept moving the piece forward, but he didn't have to carry it any longer. In fact, he seemed to be getting bigger and bigger with each space he landed in.

"Well, I don't want to get *too* big," thought Treehorn. So he moved the piece ahead slowly from one space to the next, getting bigger with each space, until he was his own regular size again. Then he put the spinner and the pieces and the instructions and the board back in the box for THE *BIG* GAME FOR KIDS TO GROW ON and put it in his closet. If he ever wanted to get bigger or smaller he could play it again, even if it *was* a pretty boring game.

Treehorn went down for breakfast and started to read the new cereal box. It said you could send for a hundred balloons. His mother was cleaning the living room. She came into the kitchen to get a dust rag.

"Don't put your elbows on the table while you're eating, dear," she said.

"Look," said Treehorn. "I'm my own size now. My own regular size."

"That's nice, dear," said Treehorn's mother. "It's a very nice size, I'm sure, and if I were you I wouldn't shrink anymore. Be sure to tell your father when he comes home tonight. He'll be so pleased." She went back to the living room and started to dust and vacuum.

That night Treehorn was watching TV. As he reached over to change channels, he noticed that his hand was bright green. He looked in the mirror that was hanging over the television set. His face was green. His ears were green. His hair was green. He was green all over.

Treehorn sighed. "I don't think I'll tell anyone," he thought to himself. "If I don't say anything, they won't notice."

Treehorn's mother came in. "Do turn the volume down a little, dear," she said. "Your father and I are having the Smedleys over to play bridge. Do comb your hair before they come, won't you, dear," said his mother as she walked back to the kitchen.

After recess, Treehorn was thirsty, so he went down the hall to the water bubbler. He couldn't reach it, and he tried to jump up high enough. He still couldn't get a drink, but he kept jumping up and down, trying.

His teacher walked by. "Why, Treehorn," she said. "That isn't like you, jumping up and down in the hall. Just because you're shrinking, it does not mean you have special privileges. What if all the children in the *school* started jumping up and down in the halls? I'm afraid you'll have to go to the Principal's office, Treehorn."

So Treehorn went to the Principal's office.

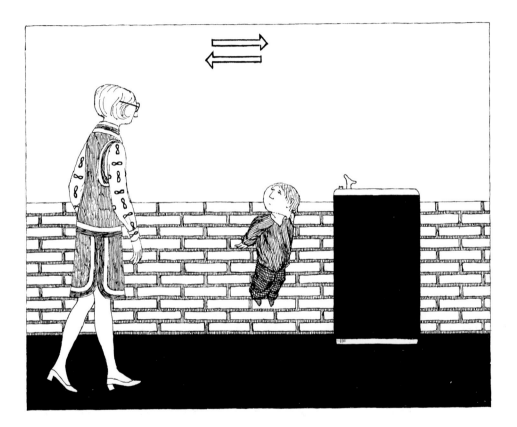

"I'm supposed to see the Principal," said Treehorn to the lady in the Principal's outer office.

"It's a very busy day," said the lady. "Please check here on this form the reason you have to see him. That will save time. Be sure to put your name down, too. That will save time. And write clearly. That will save time."

Treehorn looked at the form:

CHECK REASON YOU HAVE TO
SEE PRINCIPAL *(that will save time)*
☐ 1. Talking in class
☐ 2. Chewing gum in class
☐ 3. Talking back to teacher
☐ 4. Unexcused absence
☐ 5. Unexcused illness
☐ 6. Unexcused behavior

P.T.O.

There were many things to check, but Treehorn couldn't find one that said "Being Too Small to Reach the Water Bubbler." He finally wrote in "SHRINKING."

When the lady said he could see the Principal, Treehorn went into the Principal's office with his form.

The Principal looked at the form, and then he looked at Treehorn. Then he looked at the form again.

"I can't read this," said the Principal. "It looks like SHIRKING. You're not SHIRKING, are you, Treehorn? We can't have any shirkers here, you know. We're a team, and we all have to do our very best."

"It says SHRINKING," said Treehorn. "I'm shrinking."

"Shrinking, eh?" said the Principal. "Well, now, I'm very sorry to hear that, Treehorn. You were right to come to me. That's what I'm here for. To guide. Not to punish, but to guide. To guide all the members of my team. To solve all their problems."

"But I don't have any problems," said Treehorn. "I'm just shrinking."

"Well, I want you to know I'm right here when you need me, Treehorn," said the Principal, "and I'm glad I was here to help you. A team is only as good as its coach, eh?"

The Principal stood up. "Goodbye, Treehorn. If you have any more problems, come straight to me, and I'll help you again. A problem isn't a problem once it's solved, right?"

By the end of the day Treehorn was still smaller.

At the dinner table that night he sat on several cushions so he could be high enough to see over the top of the table.

"He's still shrinking," sniffed Treehorn's mother. "Heaven knows I've *tried* to be a good mother."

"Maybe we should call a doctor," said Treehorn's father.

"I did," said Treehorn's mother. "I called every doctor in the Yellow Pages. But no one knew anything about shrinking problems."

She sniffed again. "Maybe he'll just keep getting smaller and smaller until he disappears."

"No one disappears," said Treehorn's father positively.

"That's right, they don't," said Treehorn's mother more cheerfully. "But no one shrinks, either," she said after a moment. "Finish your carrots, Treehorn."

The next morning Treehorn was so small he had to jump out of bed. On the floor under the bed was a game he'd pushed under there and forgotten about. He walked under the bed to look at it.

It was one of the games he'd sent in for from a cereal box. He had started playing it a couple of days ago, but he hadn't had a chance to finish it because his mother had called him to come right downstairs that minute and have his breakfast or he'd be late for school.

Treehorn looked at the cover of the box:

THE *BIG* GAME
FOR KIDS TO GROW ON
IT'S TREMENDOUS! IT'S DIFFERENT!
IT'S FUN! IT'S EASY! IT'S COLOSSAL!

PLAY IT WITH FRIENDS!

PLAY IT ALONE!

Complete with Spinner, Board, Pieces,
and—!
COMPLETE INSTRUCTIONS!

The game was called THE *BIG* GAME FOR KIDS TO GROW ON.

Treehorn sat under the bed to finish playing the game.

He always liked to finish things, even if they were boring. Even if he was watching a boring program on TV, he always watched it right to the end. Games were the same way. He'd finish this one now. Where had he left off? He remembered he'd just had to move his piece back seven spaces on the board when his mother had called him.

He was so small now that the only way he could move the spinner was by kicking it, so he kicked it. It stopped at number 4. That meant he could move his piece ahead four spaces on the board.

The only way he could move the piece forward now was by carrying it, so he carried it. It was pretty heavy. He walked along the board to the fourth space. It said CONGRATULATIONS, AND UP YOU GO: ADVANCE THIRTEEN SPACES.

Treehorn started to carry his piece forward the thirteen spaces, but the piece seemed to be getting smaller. Or else *he* was getting *bigger*. That was it, he *was* getting bigger, because the bottom of the bed was getting close to his head. He pulled the game out from under the bed to finish playing it.

He kept moving the piece forward, but he didn't have to carry it any longer. In fact, he seemed to be getting bigger and bigger with each space he landed in.

"Well, I don't want to get *too* big," thought Treehorn. So he moved the piece ahead slowly from one space to the next, getting bigger with each space, until he was his own regular size again. Then he put the spinner and the pieces and the instructions and the board back in the box for THE *BIG* GAME FOR KIDS TO GROW ON and put it in his closet. If he ever wanted to get bigger or smaller he could play it again, even if it *was* a pretty boring game.

Treehorn went down for breakfast and started to read the new cereal box. It said you could send for a hundred balloons. His mother was cleaning the living room. She came into the kitchen to get a dust rag.

"Don't put your elbows on the table while you're eating, dear," she said.

"Look," said Treehorn. "I'm my own size now. My own regular size."

"That's nice, dear," said Treehorn's mother. "It's a very nice size, I'm sure, and if I were you I wouldn't shrink anymore. Be sure to tell your father when he comes home tonight. He'll be so pleased." She went back to the living room and started to dust and vacuum.

That night Treehorn was watching TV. As he reached over to change channels, he noticed that his hand was bright green. He looked in the mirror that was hanging over the television set. His face was green. His ears were green. His hair was green. He was green all over.

Treehorn sighed. "I don't think I'll tell anyone," he thought to himself. "If I don't say anything, they won't notice."

Treehorn's mother came in. "Do turn the volume down a little, dear," she said. "Your father and I are having the Smedleys over to play bridge. Do comb your hair before they come, won't you, dear," said his mother as she walked back to the kitchen.